This book belongs to:

....

EUGENE
THE GORILLA WHO WASN'T SO MEAN

by SUNNY GRIFFIN
ILLUSTRATED BY R.M. KOLDING

LANDOLL
Ashland, Ohio 44805

Eugene the gorilla walked slowly
through the jungle grass so high.
With every step he took...
out came a lonely sigh.

He said out loud to himself,
"all I wanted was a lot of friends.
With my new name I thought
everyone would come out of their dens.

EUGENE

It just may be the way I look . . . all hairy and mean.
I'm really not that way and I would never cause a scene.

I'm big and hairy, it's true" . . .
just then he heard the words,
"I'll come play with you."

Eugene looked all around and couldn't see a thing.
Maybe it's the wind, he thought, through the trees it did sing.

When suddenly he felt a
little tug on his big hairy arm.
"I'm not afraid" . . . the voice said,
"to me there will be no harm.

In order to have friends, you must be one too . . .
If you want to know how, I can teach you."

Eugene was shocked, you must know,
to see the little smart monkey with
no name, in the grass below.

"Oh, would you . . .
oh, could you please?"
said big Eugene,
now down on his knees.

EUGENE

"Edsel the elephant and Edgar the lion
have both gone on their way . . .
I'm left all alone again with no one to play."

The little smart monkey with no name said,
"Stay right here" . . .
while across the tops of the
trees he did sheer.

EUGENE

All the while calling his
monkey friends of three . . .
saying, "come quickly
and talk with me."

From out of nowhere the three did appear . . .
happily smiling from ear to ear.

"We must plan a big, fun party today.
To help Eugene meet and make friends,
it's a wonderful way."

When told, Eugene the gorilla
was so excited he couldn't stand still . . .
he laughed at the thought until
his eyes with tears did fill.

He stopped and said to his monkey friends
in a voice with a very sad sound,
"but, no one will come if I am around."

"Everyone loves a party,"
said the monkeys three . . .
"Just wait, they'll come, you'll see!"

The party was planned
and invitations were sent!
The jungle was all a buzz
wondering for who the
special party was meant.

Pretty decorations were made and hung
for everyone to see.
The little monkeys were all as busy
as they could be.

**Party day came and everything
was in its proper place . . .
the only thing sad was
the look on Eugene's face.**

But for Eugene, the no name monkey
had gone out of his way . . .
he had told the king of the jungle
all about this important day.

The old king was so pleased,
he had put out a
special decree . . .
it told everyone
on this day
where they
should be.

From out of their dens they all did come . . .
Eugene the gorilla had never had so much fun.

He met and played with all in sight.
Not one left or even acted like he might.

After the party, no one cared
that Eugene was big, hairy
and looked quite mean.
It was the beautiful inside
of him they all had seen.

Now, tell me before I go . . .
is there a special someone
you should get to know?